# THOR

## THE THUNDER CAT

# VeraLee Wiggins

**Pacific Press® Publishing Association**
Nampa, Idaho
Oshawa, Ontario, Canada

Edited by Jerry D. Thomas
Designed by Dennis Ferree
Cover art by Mary Rumford
Inside art by Kim Justinen

Wiggins, VeraLee, 1928-
    Thor the thunder cat / by VeraLee Wiggins
        p.   cm.
    Summary: As Todd helps his Siamese kitten Thor
grow into a healthy and mischievous cat, he makes
discoveries about responsibility and God's love for all his
creatures.
    ISBN 0-8163-1703-8 (alk. paper)
    [1. Cats.   2. Pets.   3. Christian life.]   I. Title.
II. Series.
PZ7.W6386Th   1999
—dc21                                          98-50008
                                                   CIP
                                                    AC

99 00 01 02 03 • 5 4 3 2 1

# Contents

# Other Books in the Julius and Friends Series

# Dedication

To Michaela Marie Wiggins
on her first birthday.
She is the daughter
of the Thunder Cat's owner,
and granddaughter of the late author.

"This kitten needs me," Todd said.

# CHAPTER

# *1*

# Shoveling Snow for a Kitten

Todd Keane put the lightweight snow shovel back into the garage. Then he sat down in the rocker on his front porch and pulled off his boots. A long white cloud formed in front of his face when he exhaled. The cold crept right through his mittens, stocking cap, and even his parka. But it didn't matter! He had just earned $12, an old Volkswagon Beetle hood, and something even more special than money.

Mr. Altman hadn't been able to come up with the money for shoveling his driveway and walks, so he had offered Todd a kitten. A Siamese kitten! Todd knew those cats cost a lot more than the two dollars he charged for shoveling snow. A lot more than he had earned all together! *Now if Mom and Dad will only let me keep it*, he thought.

Shoving his boots into a corner of the porch, Todd hurried into the house. As soon as he shut the door, his mouth started watering. And his stomach gave a couple of loud growls. "Smells great," he said. "What is it?"

"Homemade vegetable soup," Dad said. He and Mom busily washed, scraped, and cut all kinds of vegetables.

"When will it be ready?" Todd asked.

"Not for more than an hour," Mom said. "How about an apple to tide you over?"

As Todd ate the crunchy fruit, he told them about his day. Especially Mr. Altman's offer of the kitten. "You will let me have the cat, won't you?" he asked. "I worked hard, and you said we could have a pet when we were old enough to be kind to it. Molly's eight now. We both know how to treat animals. And Siamese cats are worth a bundle."

Dad and Mom looked at each other. "We'll talk about it," Dad said. "Why don't you go take a shower and get cleaned up?"

Todd shoved in the last bite of apple. Tossing the core into the trash, he tore down the hall to his bedroom.

He could hardly wait for the blessing to be over that night. While Dad thanked God out loud for the food, Todd prayed inside for the Siamese kitten. "What about the kitten?" he asked almost before Dad said Amen.

"Who'll be responsible for it?" Mom asked.

"I will," Todd said.

"Who's getting a kitten?" Molly yelled. "I want one too."

"Not this time, sweetie," Dad said. He spread margarine over a crusty brown roll and handed it to her. "This kitten is Todd's pay for shoveling someone's snow."

Molly didn't look all that happy, but she didn't say any more.

"After we finish eating, I guess we could go take a look," Dad said. "But both of you will have to remember that a kitten is not a toy. It's a real little creature that God created, with feelings and needs of its own."

After Dad agreed to look at the kitten, Todd couldn't eat another bite. He wiggled around in his chair. He shoved his food around on his plate. And he thought about Siamese cats. He had seen that man's mother cat and really liked her. Her body was the color of a deer, and she had a black face, black feet, and a black tail.

Finally the Keane family stood on Mr. Altman's porch. Todd felt so excited he almost couldn't find the doorbell. "Well, hello, Todd," Mr. Altman said when he opened the door. "Come in. I wondered if you would come back."

Mr. Altman led them to an old sofa in a back room and tipped it back. The seat went up so they could see under. There amid soft towels in a sort of a drawer lay the mother cat. She and two almost completely white kittens stared back at the Keane family through bright blue eyes. The kittens had only a few dark hairs on their faces, tails, and feet.

Todd fell in love at first glance. "I want one," he said softly.

"They are darling," Mom whispered. "May we touch?"

"In a minute," Mr. Altman said. He

turned to Todd. "How much were you charging for that job this afternoon?" he asked.

"Two dollars."

"Do you have any idea how much Siamese kittens are worth?"

Todd shook his head. "More than that."

"About twenty-five times more than that." Suddenly his smile didn't look all that friendly. "But here's what I'm going to do," his growly voice added. He reached into the open sofa and pulled out a kitten that Todd hadn't even noticed. It looked about half the size of the other two—and different. Its dull white fur looked scruffy and thin, showing the pink skin and every rib beneath. The backbone stuck out like a pencil lying on the tiny body. "This cat will be perfectly all right if it gets some decent care," he said. "The only thing wrong with it is that it's hungry. Its big brother and sister have been hogging all the food."

He handed the mewling bit of life to Todd. Todd looked at Mom in shock. The other two kittens were beautiful. This one was . . . well . . . *ugly* was the nicest word he could think of.

Todd looked down at the sad-looking kitten in his hand, and its clear blue eyes met his. It opened its mouth to cry, but no sound came out.

Then he looked again at the fat, sleek kittens in the sofa box. Their mother was giving them a bath with her rough pink tongue, and he could hear them purring.

He looked at the one in his hand and found it still gazing into his eyes. Those kittens were happy, but this poor, starving little thing didn't know what the word meant. Suddenly something strange happened to Todd's heart. It swelled almost out of his chest with love for the ugly, runty, scruffy-looking animal. He'd make this kitten live. He'd make it happy too. Even happier than those big, beautiful kittens under the couch.

"I want it, Mom," he said. "This one needs me."

Mom looked at Dad. "Think it'll live?"

He shook his head. "I'm not sure, but it'll have a better chance if we take it than it will here."

"Just give it lots of warm food," the man said, "and before you know it, it'll catch up with the others."

They took the kitten home and offered it a bowl of warm milk. But it wouldn't drink.

"Where's your doll bottle?" Todd asked Molly. "I think it needs a bottle." Molly ran after her toy, and the kitten snatched the nipple as if it had been taking a bottle all its life.

"I want to feed it," Molly said. "It's my bottle."

"No way," Todd answered. "You're too little."

"I'm not, either." She snatched at the kitten, but Todd jerked it away.

"Stop!" Dad said in a loud voice. "Give the kitten to Mom, Todd." Mom cradled it in her arms and gently put the bottle back into its mouth.

"Todd and Molly, you're both acting like wild animals snatching at food," Dad went on. "Even if that kitten were a cookie, you would be acting badly. But it has feelings and must be handled gently. Neither of you is acting mature enough to care for a pet."

He walked from the room without another word.

The doll's baby bottle was just right
for feeding the kitten.

# CHAPTER

# 2

# As Strong as Thunder

Todd looked at Molly. She looked about as sad as he felt. Dad was right. They had both been really bad and had mistreated the kitten. No one said a word for a long time. The tiny kitten made the only sound, sucking the milk from the bottle.

"Look," Mom finally said as the kitten kept sucking. "See its little feet pumping against the bottle? That means it's happy."

Both children crowded close to watch. Todd could see little bubbles in the bottle. "May I hold it now?" he asked.

"It's my turn!" Molly said.

Mom shook her head. "You haven't

learned a thing, have you?" She looked disappointed for a moment. "It's your kitten, Todd," she finally said. "If you can behave, you can feed it. If I hear one more outburst from either of you, we'll take the kitten right back where we got it." She placed the tiny creature in Todd's arms so carefully that it didn't know it had been moved.

Todd felt his heart fill with love as the kitten gulped the milk down. He would take good care of it. In fact, he would help it be the biggest and strongest cat in the neighborhood. As he stroked its little forehead with one finger, he heard a noise and looked up. Molly sat sobbing in Dad's recliner, her head on the armrest.

Todd suddenly knew how he would feel if the kitten were hers and he couldn't touch it. Awful. The kitten finished the bottle and didn't even open its eyes. Todd found a little cardboard box. Wrapping the kitten in a towel, he laid it ever so gently in the box.

He went back into the living room, where Molly still cried. "Would you like to play with me?" he asked quietly.

She lifted her tear-stained face. "Play what?" she asked.

"Whatever you want." He almost held his breath, wondering what dumb thing he would be playing.

Molly brushed the tears from her face and jumped down from the chair. "Dolls!" she shouted. "I'll get them."

Todd groaned inside but kept his smile pasted on his face. He owed Molly one. He wanted to make her happy as well as the kitten.

Molly returned a moment later with four dolls and a big box of clothes. She handed him two dolls. "Get them ready for church," she said. "We don't want to be late."

Todd shoved the dolls into dresses and shoes.

"Now, bring them to church," she said. When they had the dolls all lined up, sitting on the carpet, one of Molly's dolls led the singing—several choruses they both knew. Todd helped his dolls sing.

Then Molly's other doll preached a sermon about how God loves the little birds and animals. And how He loves us even more.

Todd listened quietly, surprised at his little sister's—no, at the doll's understanding of Jesus' love. After the sermon, the dolls filed silently from the "church."

"Would you come to my house for lunch?" Molly's singing doll asked Todd's doll.

"How come you don't have any boy dolls?" Todd asked.

"I don't like boys," Molly answered, flipping her nose into the air. "Boys are gross." She walked away, humming "Jesus Loves Me."

At worship that night, everyone prayed for the kitten to grow strong. Todd also prayed for help to be a nicer big brother. Then he took the kitten to his room so he could feed it when it woke up during the night.

And it seemed to Todd that he had barely fallen asleep when the kitten started its weak crying. He fed it a bottle, cleaned the bottle, and fell back into bed.

The same thing happened several more

times during the night. The last few times, Todd didn't remember whether he cleaned the bottle or not. The next morning, he felt almost too tired to go to school. He wondered if having a cat was really worth the trouble. But then he saw its little chest rise and fall with each tiny breath. And he noticed its round little tummy. He felt proud that he had taken care of its needs. He felt something else too—a love so strong for the helpless little animal that his breath came quickly. He would help that kitten grow bigger and happier than its piggy brothers. Or sisters.

"What are you naming the kitten?" Dad asked at the breakfast table.

Todd thought a moment. "I don't know if it's a boy or a girl," he finally said. "How can I name it until I find out?"

"It's a boy," Dad said. "A tiny, helpless, weak little boy cat that may not even live."

Todd didn't have to think for one second. "He'll live," he said. "And his name is Thor. A long time ago people in Norway called the thunder Thor, and my cat's going to be as strong as thunder."

That afternoon when Todd came home from school, Mom told him she had fed Thor three bottles. "If he keeps on eating like that, he'll be Thor, all right," she said with a smile.

Todd gave Thor another bottle then shot some baskets in the driveway with his family. But he kept thinking about his new little kitten. He had played only about an hour when he decided to quit. Thor might need something, and he was all alone in the house.

When they went outside, Thor was trying to climb out of his box and crying for food. Todd warmed the milk, tested it on his arm, and handed the bottle to Molly. She sat in the rocker and held the bottle carefully so Thor wouldn't swallow air and get a tummyache. "Come quick," she yelled a moment later.

Todd rushed to her side and immediately heard a loud, raspy sound as the kitten's feet pumped against the bottle in Molly's hand. "He's purring!" Todd said. "Now he's happy, like the other kittens."

That night, Thor succeeded in climbing

out of his box, so Mom brought in a litter box and put the kitten into it. He sniffed all over the box, pawed at the litter, then turned around twice and made a tiny little puddle. "Good boy," Todd said. "That's a really good kitten." He petted the kitten until it purred.

Whenever Thor escaped from his box, someone put him into the litter box. He usually did what they wanted him to.

One afternoon Mom, Todd, and Molly came home from the supermarket and began putting groceries away. As they emptied each bag, they dropped it on the floor. They would fold and put them away when they finished. Thor spotted the paper bags scattered over the kitchen floor. He scampered into one of them and turned around so he could see out. As Todd walked past, the tiny little animal zapped from the bag and attacked his ankle.

April Fool!

# CHAPTER

# 3

# April Fools'!

Todd looked down at the little cat scratching and clawing at his ankle. He laughed and leaned down to pet Thor, but the kitten jumped off his ankle and back into the bag.

"He thinks he's a hermit crab," Todd said. "He just found himself a shell."

As the days passed, Thor outgrew his little box. He climbed onto the couch for his daytime naps and slept with Todd at night. One afternoon, Todd stepped into the living room and found the kitten all stretched out on the couch. "I can tell whether it's hot or cold by watching Thor sleep," he told Mom. "When it's cold he curls all up in a little ball. He even tucks his nose into his fur. When it's hot he stretches out as long as he can."

Mom nodded. "I hadn't thought about it, but that's exactly what he does."

The kitten had more than doubled his size. His fur had changed from a thin, rough pink to snow white to a shiny, thick, pale cream color. His nose, ears, feet, and tail had some brown hairs coming in. *God must really have fun deciding on color combinations for all His animals,* Todd thought. *For sure, He always came up with perfect colors.*

"When do you think I can stop giving Thor bottles during the night?" Todd asked one evening after worship. "He still gets me up every night."

Dad laughed. "One thing for sure, Todd. You've proven to be a good father."

"He should be able to go all night now," Mom said. "I think he's spoiled."

"Why don't we start giving him cat food?" Molly asked. "He could eat that by himself if he got hungry."

Everyone thought that was a great idea,

so after a trip to the grocery store, Todd put a jar lid filled with canned kitty tuna on his bedroom floor against the wall. "I'll just put him over there when he gets hungry," Todd said. "In a couple of days he'll get it by himself."

Todd gave Thor a bottle and took him to bed that night. But the kitten didn't wait for Todd to show him the tuna. He scrambled right out of bed and ran to it. He ate all he could hold and then sat over the food. After a while he fell asleep, and his chin dropped into the tuna. He jerked awake, ate a few bites and then sat there until he fell asleep again.

Todd carried the greedy kitten to bed three times, but Thor wanted the tuna so badly he couldn't leave it. "I got less sleep than ever," Todd grumbled in the morning. "That cat's such a pig he tried to stay awake all night."

Finally he decided to give Thor his canned food in the daytime and dry food at night. It worked, and before long Thor got a bottle only when someone felt like giving him one. But he still got plenty of bottles.

He had learned to hold his own bottle with all four little feet. Everyone thought it was so cute, so they kept giving him bottles.

Mom had two orange trees, one grapefruit tree, and one lemon tree in the living room beside the big windows. One evening, Thor decided he was old enough to climb trees. He chose the smallest, the grapefruit, which stood about five feet tall. "Hey!" Molly said, "Thor's in the tree."

Todd's eyes jerked to the tree in time to see the limb waving like crazy. As Todd watched, the cat fell from the upper side of the branch. He clung to the flapping limb with all four feet, his body swinging underneath. Finally Todd managed to get himself together and caught the kitten before he fell to the carpet. Thor snuggled close to Todd for fifteen minutes. He trembled as if he had nearly fallen from a tall pine tree.

"You should have let him fall," Molly said. "Mommy doesn't want him to wreck her trees."

Mom looked up from her crossword puzzle. Her eyes twinkled. "I don't think he'll climb the trees too often," she said.

"Remember the thorns?"

Todd nodded. He remembered the thorns, all right. Whenever he and Molly got balloons, the trees popped them. Todd decided to watch his cat even more carefully. Those trees would pop Thor if he messed around with them much.

One morning Todd crawled from his bed, trying not to wake Thor. But as usual, the cat tore out through the door about the time Todd's feet hit the floor beside his bed. Todd pulled on a sock and then shoved his foot into a shoe. *Crack!* When he pulled his foot out, eggshell clung to his sock, as well as yellow and clear, slimy stuff.

Molly jumped into the room laughing so hard she held her sides. "April Fool!" she yelled then collapsed onto Todd's bed in gales of laughter. Todd didn't find it quite as funny as Molly, but he had to admit it was a good trick. He had forgotten that it was April 1—April Fools' Day.

He grinned at her. "Good trick. Now, how about helping me clean up the mess before Mom sees the carpet?" They cleaned the carpet together. Then he took his sneaker to the bathroom and washed it out. After drying the inside the best he could with a washcloth, he put it on. It felt only a little squishy.

After breakfast, he found his windbreaker hood strings tied together. "April Fool!" Molly yelled.

Todd came home from school that day ready for a rest from April Fool tricks. He played with Thor awhile. Then Dad came home, and they played a basketball game before supper.

After supper, he walked into the living room and picked Thor off the couch. The cat's face had turned blue! What could have happened to him? He raced into the kitchen with the kitten. "Something's wrong with Thor!" he yelled.

Mom turned to look at the kitten, her face wearing a puzzled look. Todd held Thor gently in his arms, looking at his pet's face. He felt his heart in his throat. "Something awful must be wrong to turn Thor's face all blue," he squeaked. He felt tears behind his eyes. He pleaded with God to make his kitten be all right.

"April Fool!" Molly yelled, laughing so hard she had to drop into a chair.

"What do you mean?" Mom asked. She laid down her dish towel and took the kitten. Then she turned to Molly. "What did you do to this cat, young lady?"

"I put blue food—food"—she could hardly speak through her laughter—"coloring on his food," she finally finished.

Todd's face turned bright red. He grabbed his little sister and held her arms—hard. "What were you trying to do, kill him?" He bellowed. "How do you know that food coloring won't hurt him really bad? I'm sick of you and your dumb April Fools' stuff!"

Thor wants to play croquet.

# CHAPTER

## 4

## Croquet Disaster

Todd's face grew redder, and his breath came hard. He just felt so upset with his little sister he couldn't stand it. How could she hurt an innocent little animal, anyway? How would she like it if some huge creature mistreated her? Finally, he gave her a big push, and she fell to the floor.

She lay there for a moment, her blue eyes wide, then started to cry. "I didn't want Thor to feel left out." She sobbed. "Everyone else was playing April Fool, and I didn't want him to feel bad."

Mom pulled the little girl onto her lap. "I understand why you did it, Molly," she said in a loving voice. "But you shouldn't have. Animals don't understand games and tricks. It probably won't make Thor sick, but you're just a little girl and can't be sure about those things."

"Tell her she can never touch Thor again," Todd yelled. "Ever!" He rushed into the bathroom with the kitten, slamming the door as hard as he could. Setting the cat on the counter, he pulled out a clean washcloth and soaked it with warm water. He scrubbed the kitten's face carefully, several times. But the kitten looked just as blue when he finished as when he started.

When Molly finally ran off to play, Mom called Todd. "Your kitten is a sealpoint Siamese," she said. Then she chuckled. "You can look at Thor now and have an idea how he'd look if he were a blue point." She laughed out loud, as if she'd pulled an April Fools' trick herself.

That night Mom called Todd into her room after Molly had fallen asleep. "Thor's all right," she said. "He'd have been sick by now if the food coloring had affected him."

"Good," Todd said. "Molly's the worst

brat I ever saw."

Mom shook her head. "No, she isn't." Then she smiled at him. "I've always thought the worst brats slammed doors. Molly's just trying to grow up, Todd. She didn't want to hurt Thor. And if you had quietly explained why she shouldn't have messed with his food, she'd have understood her error just as well. Usually you can teach people without making them feel bad." Her eyes rolled toward the ceiling. "Or getting physical. That's never right. And it's against the rules in this house, but I'm going to let you decide how to make it right."

The next day after school, Molly told Todd she was sorry she had messed up Thor's face. "I promise I'll never do anything bad to him again," she said, crossing her heart on her chest.

"Thanks," Todd said. "I'm sorry I pushed you. I shouldn't have. I'm trying to treat you better." He grinned. "It's hard, but I really am trying."

After supper that night, Molly edged up to Todd. She held a tiny pair of blue pajamas in her hand. "Would it hurt Thor if I dressed him in doll clothes?" she asked.

Todd raised his eyebrows at Mom.

Mom smiled. "The clothes won't hurt him if they're not too small. But you might hurt him putting them on him."

Molly brought the pajamas to Mom. "You show me how."

Mom took the kitten and the pajamas. "They'll fit fine," she said. Then she started carefully pulling them over Thor's feet. "The main thing is never bend his legs back. Just hold the clothes below his normal leg position and slip them over. Animals' legs won't bend out as people's arms do." She finished snapping the tiny garment over the kitten's back and set him on the floor.

The kitten stood on four feet a moment then fell over on his side on the carpet. Everyone laughed. Todd put him on his feet again. Thor fell again.

"Leave him alone," Dad whispered. "He'll figure out he's OK." Thor lay flat for a few moments and then gathered himself together and stood up. He looked so long and skinny and funny in the clothes that everyone burst into laughter.

Thor raised his head high and ran across the room. When he reached Todd, he stopped, took one last look at his pajamas, and jumped into Todd's lap. Curling himself into a little ball, he fell asleep. Molly gently took off the pajamas so Thor could sleep better.

Thor interrupted worship that night, meowing loudly. Todd went after the cat and tucked him over his shoulder. Thor seemed delighted but soon slipped away and started his yowling again. Todd found him on the bed and brought him back to the living room, where Dad waited patiently to continue the story from *Primary Treasure.*

After the third time, Dad asked Todd what was going on. "He wants to go to bed," Todd said. "He doesn't know he can go alone."

"Well," Dad said, "I've never heard such a horrible sound."

"I have," Mom said. "All Siamese cats howl like that, Dad. You may as well get used to it. Thor will get it down pat one of these days, and people a block away will hear." She smiled at Todd. "Some people refuse to have Siamese cats because they can't stand their yowling."

Dad grinned and put his hands over his ears. "I might be one of them," he said. "Go put him in your room, Todd, and shut the door so we can finish worship."

"Now I know why his name's Thor," Molly said, laughing. "He's louder than thunder."

One evening after supper, the family decided to play a game of croquet. Thor followed them into the backyard and chased small insects he found in the lawn. "Don't let him eat those bugs!" Molly screamed when she noticed.

Todd grinned. He had been watching and felt certain Thor wouldn't eat the bugs. "What's the matter, Molly?" he asked. "Don't you know that bugs have lots of protein?"

After Molly figured out the cat wasn't eating anything gross, she and Todd started setting up wickets and stakes. Then they all chose their mallets and balls. Molly chose red because red plays first. Todd chose yellow so he could play second. The object of the game is to knock the balls across the lawn through the wickets to the stakes at the end. Then you do the same backward. The first one back to the beginning wins the game.

Molly knocked her ball through two wickets, screaming with delight. When she tried again, the ball missed the wicket and rolled past.

Then Todd put his ball through the first two and also the next.

Mom and Dad took their turns, but both missed. Then Molly played again and caught up with Todd. In fact, her ball touched his. "I'm going to knock his ball out of the lawn," Molly said, wearing a big grin.

Dad shook his head. "Better not. He might do it to you, and you'll cry." (In croquet, if your ball touches another, you can put your foot on your ball and then hit your own ball. That makes the other ball fly away.)

Molly laughed. "He won't catch me." Then she put her foot on her ball and hit it as hard as she could. Todd's yellow ball jumped ten feet across the lawn—right into Thor's little black face. The kitten slumped to the ground.

Molly dropped her mallet and ran to the quiet kitten. "I've killed Thor!" she screamed. "I've killed our very first little kitty."

Todd picked up his injured pet.

# CHAPTER
# 5

# Miracle Cat

Molly cried so hard Mom took her into the house. Dad stayed with Todd. Taking the still kitten from Todd, he examined the tiny body. First, he felt over the kitten's head gently but thoroughly. After checking every part of the animal, he shook his head. "I don't know exactly what's wrong, but he's badly hurt."

Just then, Mom and Molly came back out. Molly's eyes looked red, but she wasn't crying anymore. "We've been praying for him," Molly said. "We want you to pray with us. Mommy says the Bible says for us all to pray together."

The entire family knelt under a large weeping willow tree, and each asked God to heal the little animal. After they finished, they walked quietly indoors, leaving Todd alone with Thor.

Less than a minute later, Thor shuddered all over. All four of his legs trembled a moment. Then he looked up at Todd. He shook his head and sat up in Todd's arms.

"He's awake!" Todd yelled, running into the house to the utility room. He set the kitten on the floor, and Thor walked steadily to the food dish and ate a few bites. Then he sat down and looked up at Todd. His mouth opened, and that horrible Siamese yowl ripped through the entire house.

That night during worship, every member of the Keane family thanked their heavenly Father for making their kitten well. Todd thanked Him again after he climbed into bed. He felt certain he had just seen a miracle.

Thor slept well, and the next morning he seemed as good as new.

One sunny Sunday about two weeks later, Dad announced that it was time to put in the garden. Molly acted as though Dad had suggested an outing to the beach, but Todd didn't feel all that eager. He had been looking forward to working on his bicycle exhaust system.

His friend Marco came over about the time Todd plodded out to the garden. Marco offered to help.

Todd grinned. "Sure. If you don't mind being bored."

Molly and Mom planted beans on the other side of the garden.

Dad gave Todd a cottage cheese carton full of corn kernels. "One of you make the trench," he said, wiping sweat from his forehead with his dusty hand, "and the other can drop the corn in. Or however you want." He went back to work with Mom and Molly.

"I'll make the trench," Marco said, picking up the hoe. He started pulling the hoe through the soft earth, making a nice ditch.

Todd wasn't very excited about messing around in the warm dirt, but Thor didn't feel that way at all. He raced around in circles, stopping to scratch wildly in the ground. Then he took off in a big circle again, having the time of his life. Todd sat on the ground, watching his pet, loving the kitten's excitement. Sure, the kitten could have fun. He didn't have to plant corn.

"Come on, Todd," Marco yelled. "I have the trenches all finished. Drop in the corn so I can cover them up." Todd finally got his feet under him and started dropping in corn. One kernel every six inches.

Todd planted row after row of corn, and Marco covered it behind him. Finally, Todd checked his corn seeds and decided it was like the Bible story of the widow's jug of oil; the more he planted, the more he had left. No way could the family eat all that corn. He dropped in another kernel, and Thor jumped on it, digging around it furiously.

When the kitten pranced away, Todd couldn't see the corn anymore. "Hey," he said to Marco, who followed close behind, "Thor covered up the last one. How about you dropping them in and letting Thor cover them? I'm tired."

"How are you doing?" Dad yelled from across the garden before Marco could answer. "About finished with the corn? I have some other seeds you two can plant when you finish."

Todd plopped right down in the soft earth. Why should he hurry if there was no end to his work? Anyway, it was getting hot.

He looked at his carton of seeds. Still almost half full. He took a quick look around, and everyone but Marco was busy. "Hey, Marco," Todd called. "Could you go fill Thor's dish with water? And be sure to take him with you so he can drink. I don't want him to get sick in this hot sun."

As soon as Marco cradled the kitten in his arms and headed toward the house, Todd grabbed the hoe and dug a big, deep hole. He quickly looked around to make sure no one was watching. He dumped all the seeds into the hole and shoved the dirt over them. Then he stomped the ground down.

"You were right," Marco said, dropping to the soft, warm earth beside Todd. "Thor drank until his tummy got round. Hey, what happened to the rest of the corn?"

"I got it all in while you were gone," Todd said. Well, he didn't tell a lie. He sure did get it in.

One day Molly asked for a pet.

"I don't think we're ready for another pet yet," Dad answered. "Can't you enjoy Thor? He can be everybody's friend."

Molly's smile turned upside down. "It isn't fair, Daddy. Todd has the best pet in the world, and I don't have any."

"What kind of pet were you thinking of, love?" Mom asked.

"I want a turtle."

Mom shuddered. Dad looked thoughtful. "Would you be happy with a turtle?" he asked.

Molly jumped up and down, clapping her hands. "Yes! Can we go to the pet store and get one right now, Daddy? Can we? Please?"

Todd worked on his exhaust system for his bike while Dad and Molly went after the turtle. He wired a piece of pipe on the bike, extending it behind the pedals. He planned to shove extrafine dust into the pipe, and when he rode, the dust would come out just right to make perfect exhaust smoke.

He hadn't finished when Dad drove into the driveway and Molly jumped from the car. "I got two turtles," she yelled, "so they won't get lonely. Come see them."

Todd laid his screwdriver down and walked slowly over to the driveway. Who cared about dumb old turtles anyway? They looked exactly as he had expected—greenish gray, with their heads and feet tucked into their shells. Ugly.

"Come on, Todd," Molly said, "help me set them up in the garage." With a loud sigh, Todd followed Molly into the garage. He looked around for a safe place to keep the turtles.

"Let's put them on the workbench," he said. "It's high enough so nothing will bother them." He picked up the small blue plastic swimming pool. "This thing must be for tiny kids," he said. It just fit on the extrawide workbench. Then he climbed a ladder to the ceiling and hooked the electric cord over an unfinished board so the light hung over the blue pool. "I hope your turtles are worth all this work," he told Molly.

The turtles find a soft place to rest.

# CHAPTER

# 6

# Catnip and Turtles

The turtles still hid inside their shells in the small box Molly had brought them home in. *Probably too dumb to come out and enjoy the nice place I made for them,* Todd thought.

"Now they need some water," Todd said. "Go ask Mom for an old cake pan or something."

Molly brought back a bent-up roaster pan about five inches deep, ten inches wide, and eighteen inches long. "Will this work?" she asked.

"Yes, but you'll have to get some rocks to help them climb into and out of the water."

In a little while the turtles' blue pool looked homey and ready for them. Molly put one into the water and one on a rock beside the pan. The one she put into the water woke up and began swimming around in its little pool.

"He likes it!" Molly squealed with excitement.

Todd nodded. The turtle did seem to like the water. "OK," he said, "I'm making something for my bike, so I'm going back outside. You'd better get something for your new pets to eat."

"The man at the pet store said they like bananas, romaine lettuce, and tuna fish," she said. "Daddy got stuff for them to eat."

"Well, then give them some." Todd took off for his bike. He finished fastening the plastic pipe really tight then stuffed some dry dust into the pipe on his bike.

Gram and Gramp's car turning into the driveway made Todd forget all about the exhaust system. "We heard you have a kitten," Gram called.

"Yes! I'll find him for you. He's really neat." Todd ran into the house for Thor.

When he returned with Thor riding on his shoulders, he noticed Gramp had some leaves in his hand.

"That's some cat," Gramp said. "I've never seen a prettier Siamese. He's going to be big too."

Gram took Thor from Todd and petted him, but the kitten seemed to shrink into himself. Each time she stroked his fur, he washed away her finger marks with his rough little tongue. She handed him back to Todd. "That cat doesn't even want me to touch him," she said, laughing. "You have him thoroughly spoiled."

"Put him on the ground," Gramp said. "I have something for him."

Todd did.

When Gramp dropped his leaves next to Thor's nose, the cat went crazy. He attacked the leaves, rolled in them, and tried to eat them. He barely rested a moment before he repeated his routine again.

"What is that stuff?" Todd asked.

Mom came outside and joined the family. They all watched Thor for another minute. Todd couldn't believe anything in the whole world could make his cat so excited.

"That's catnip," Gramp said. "I have some roots for you." He headed for his car. "That little bit will soon be wilted if your cat doesn't eat it or tear it to shreds."

Todd followed Gramp to the car and took the small paper sack. Gramp put his arm over Todd's shoulder and steered him toward the garden. "Let's go plant it right now," he said.

Todd remembered how he didn't like planting gardens, but this was different. This was for Thor.

"Let's stick them right here," Gramp said, pointing. "The ground seems extra soft."

Todd gulped. Gramp had pointed at almost the exact spot where he had buried the corn. Todd dropped to his knees and pushed the soft dirt away with his hands. He breathed a big sigh when he didn't see any of the corn kernels. Pulling the small roots from the sack, he planted them just below the surface as Gramp told him.

"Thanks a lot," he told Gramp when he finished. "Thor will have a lot of fun with the catnip when it grows." Gramp picked up a small stick and handed it to Todd. "Why don't you push this into the ground to mark the place where you planted it?"

Then Molly showed them her new pets. Gramp said he was sorry he didn't have any turtlenip for them. Gram and Gramp stayed for supper and the evening.

Molly complained when she had to go to bed. Todd felt the same way at his bedtime, but he went quietly.

Todd usually found Thor waiting for him on his bed, but tonight he wasn't even in the room. Todd did a quick search of the places he might be but couldn't find the kitten anywhere.

"Mom," he yelled from the utility room, "could you help me find Thor? I don't think he's in the house." Mom came; so did Dad, Gram, and Gramp. While the others searched the house again, Gramp and Todd went outside and called around the house and yard. Still no Thor.

Finally the group all gathered in the kitchen, wondering what to do next. "I know what happened," Todd said, his voice breaking. "Someone stole him. People like Siamese cats, and Thor is an extra-special one."

Gram told Todd that Thor was all right. "People in this neighborhood don't steal cats," she said, "even if they are Siamese and extra-special. He's just gone to sleep in some little corner. Think like a cat, Todd. Where would you hide to take a nap?"

Todd couldn't imagine. More than anything in the world, Thor loved to be warm, so he always went to Todd's bed. No place was as warm as the bed. Todd silently prayed for his furry friend. He had to be all right. He just had to.

"We've searched the entire house, lawn, and garden," Mom said. "I'm afraid he's not on the place at all."

"Say," Gramp said, "we didn't look in the garage, did we?"

Todd shook his head. "Thor never goes in the garage. He likes luxury, like carpets, upholstered furniture, and warm beds. He wouldn't be in the garage."

"Let's look anyway," Dad said. "It's our last hope." He opened the garage door and stepped through. Todd followed. Usually at night the garage was inky black, but tonight a dim light shone in the area. Todd looked around but didn't see Thor. As he neared the light, he remembered Molly's turtles. *Might as well take a peek at them,* he thought. *They might have their heads out of their shells now so I can see them.*

But when he leaned over to check the turtles, he found Thor lying directly under the light, sound asleep. Both turtles sat on top of the kitten. Todd couldn't believe his eyes. "Dad," he whispered, "come here."

Dad's eyes opened wide when he saw the kitten sleeping with the turtles. They tiptoed back into the house and got Mom, Gram, and Gramp.

"Thor went in there to get warm," Mom said. "The turtles wanted to get warm too, so they did what they had to do. They climbed on Thor to get to the light."

Todd took his cat to bed and thanked God for keeping Thor safe. Then he noticed an awful smell. It seemed to grow worse. After a while, he jumped out of bed. He took his cat to the bathroom and washed him all over with a warm, damp washcloth. He hoped that would get the turtle yuck off.

Thor's new friends.

# CHAPTER
# 7

# Stowaway Thor

One evening Molly brought her turtles in and put them on the floor. "I'm having a turtle race," she told everyone. "It'll start in five minutes, so you better come watch."

When Molly invited the family to a turtle race, Dad grinned at Mom. Mom rolled her eyes toward the ceiling. But the family went into the living room and sat on the couch. Todd sat in the rocker with Thor draped over his shoulder.

Molly put the turtles on the carpet, side by side.

"Gentlemen," Todd said in the tone of an announcer, "you may start your engines."

"Todd!" Molly scolded, "you stop that. This is my race." She put a hand behind each turtle and gave them a little push. One turtle didn't move. The other took several lumbering steps forward.

"What are your turtles' names, sugar?" Dad asked.

"The one who's racing is Pokey," she said. "And the other is Splash."

"Good names," Todd said. "Pokey's going to win."

Thor's head jerked up, and his clear blue eyes opened wide as Pokey oozed across the carpet. Then he tumbled from Todd's shoulder and pounced on the turtle. Before anyone could stop him, he lay on his back with the turtle balanced between his paws. He tossed the turtle and batted it with each paw before Molly took it from him. "Bad, bad kitty," she said, shaking her finger at Thor's sooty nose.

"When you're through playing with your turtles, be sure to wash with soap and water," Mom said.

Molly made a face. "My pets aren't fun at all," she whined. "Todd doesn't have to wash after he plays with Thor."

"He should," Dad said. "But sometimes turtles carry salmonella. If you get that disease, it's like having the flu really bad or even worse. That's why we wash with soap every time we touch them. Hey, if the race is over, let's go see how the garden's doing. Everything should be up now. The radishes might even be ready to eat."

The family went outside, Thor riding on Todd's shoulder as usual. Todd checked on the catnip first and couldn't believe the solid patch of grassy green. He put Thor down in the middle of the patch, but the cat looked at it with distaste, held up one paw, and leapt to bare ground.

"Mom," Todd called, "I planted some catnip for Thor, and he doesn't like it anymore."

Mom hurried over and looked at the grassy green patch. "That's not catnip, Todd, that's corn. I wonder how so much corn got planted in one spot."

All at once, Todd knew how it happened. The corn he had buried had grown! He hadn't thought about that happening. And where was the catnip?

Dad arrived on the scene. "I wondered why we got three fewer rows of corn than last year," he said. He raised his eyebrows at Todd.

Todd didn't want to tell that he had buried the corn, but he had a feeling Dad already knew. How could he know?

"Wonder how I know?" Dad asked. "I remember doing the same thing with beans. "Only I gave the beans a big toss. Gramp had to stick long bean stakes up all over the garden to support the beanstalks. That year I picked beans here and there, but at least we had beans. The corn is a different matter. It is so close together that it can't live. We may as well pull it out so your catnip can grow. Otherwise, we won't have anything."

Todd felt pretty strange pulling up the corn he had tried to lose. Dad could have gotten really mad about the whole thing. Todd decided he had a pretty good dad. Maybe he could make up for it by taking extra-special care of the garden.

Finally school dismissed for the summer, and the family prepared for a weekend camping trip. Dad hooked the camp trailer up to the pickup, and they loaded it with food and clothes. Every time Todd carried groceries to the trailer, Thor jumped inside. He always raced up onto the big queen bed. He lay there until Todd hauled him outside.

Every time Todd brought something more to the trailer, it happened again. Todd started wondering what they were going to do with Thor while they camped. That night he asked.

"He'll be all right while we're gone," Mom said. "We'll leave him in the basement with lots of food and water."

"Yeah," Molly chimed in. "I have to leave Splash and Pokey too."

Todd didn't feel right about leaving Thor at home, so he prayed about it that night, asking his heavenly Father to help him be able to take Thor along.

About noon the next day they started off to a little lake high in the mountains. And Todd hadn't been able to convince Mom and Dad to bring Thor. After about an hour, Molly fell asleep, so Todd sat quietly, wondering why his prayer to bring Thor hadn't been answered.

"Here we are," Dad finally said, turning into a campground. They chose a campsite; then Dad backed the trailer in and unhooked it. While he hooked up hoses and cords, Mom asked for the key so she could get into the trailer and start supper.

Dad handed her the key, which she inserted into the lock and turned. The door popped open, and Thor dashed between her feet, tearing off through the trees.

"Help!" she called. "Thor just ran off."

"Oh no!" Dad said. "He's so spooked we'll never catch him."

Todd dropped the piece of wood he had been wedging under the trailer wheels and tore off after Thor. "Come back here, you turkey!" he yelled, puffing and running as fast as he could. The faster he ran, the faster Thor ran. After running several minutes, Todd sank to the ground to rest. Peering ahead, he discovered Thor resting too. He tried to get his legs under him, but they felt exactly like pieces of string. Finally he gave up and settled on the ground. In a minute, he would be able to go again.

Todd stretched out in the shade, put an arm under his head for a pillow, and shut his eyes for just a second. A moment later he felt something sniffing at his fingers. He stiffened. What could it be? He realized that out here in the woods, it could be anything.

Afraid to move, almost afraid to open his eyes, he peeked through his lashes. But he didn't see a wild animal. He saw Thor's head pushing against his fingers. Then the cat turned his attention to Todd's face, rubbing and chirping as though they had been apart for years.

Todd jerked to a sitting position and pulled the cat onto his lap. If Thor had been scared, he had recovered, for he purred as loudly as he could, pumping his feet against Todd's leg. Suddenly Todd remembered his family. He'd better get back and tell them his pet was safe. He scrambled to his feet, Thor cradled in his arms, and trotted back to the trailer.

"Thor's all right," he called.

Dad stuck his head out. "Better get him in here quick," he said. "We might not be able to catch him if he gets away again."

Brave Thor rides in the rowboat.

# CHAPTER
# 8

# Thor Loves Camping and Cookies

Todd held Thor tenderly in his arms. His cat wasn't like other cats. "He won't run away, Dad. He's not scared." But he opened the door, stepped inside, and tossed Thor onto the high bed. The fawn-colored cat settled right down in the quilts, gave himself a quick bath, and fell asleep.

"Ready to go swimming?" Dad asked. "Get your swimsuits on, and we'll walk over to the lake."

Ten minutes later, Todd stuck a big toe into the lake. It felt like ice. "That's too cold," he said. He forced himself to go out until the water covered his knees. Then he stopped. "You may as well forget it, Molly," he called back to shore. "You could never handle this cold."

As he finished talking, a small form rushed past him, and Molly splashed head-long into the water beside him. She came up screaming and laughing. And splashing Todd.

"Stop!" Todd yelled, running back to the shore. What was the matter with that kid? Couldn't she feel the ice in the water?

Dad managed to ease out until the small waves lapped at his hips. Molly splashed him, too, and then dove into the water, swimming away from him as fast as she could.

Todd crouched at the edge of the water, trying to get warm as he watched Dad and his little sister. "I'm going back to the trailer," he called, rising to a standing position. As he turned to leave the lake, he saw Thor racing toward him. How did that cat get out of the trailer, anyway?

Thor stopped a few feet from the edge of the lake, looking across the water at Dad and Molly. Todd watched him move to the water and carefully dip one paw into the icy foam at the edge. He jerked it back as if he'd been burned. Standing in the same spot, he licked the foot dry and then bounded over to Todd and into his arms.

"At least we think alike, don't we?" Todd asked his pet as he carried him back to the trailer.

He found Mom searching for Thor. "I'm so glad you found him," she said in an excited voice. "I knew for sure he was gone forever this time."

Todd grinned. "Don't worry about Thor anymore, Mom. He only came to find us." Todd wasn't sure that God answers prayer by sending stowaways. But just in case, he thanked his heavenly Father for answering his prayer to bring Thor camping.

After that, Thor ran through the campground to suit himself. He even rode on the bow of the rowboat the family rented to explore the lake and surrounding area.

On the last night of their trip, the family had worship and prepared for bed. But Todd couldn't find Thor. "I know he's all right," he said, "but I'm tired. Sometimes he's a little too independent for me."

Dad didn't reply but seemed to be examining the inside of the trailer.

"He's not in here," Todd said. "I've looked everywhere in the trailer. There aren't many places to hide."

Dad chuckled. "I wasn't looking for Thor, Todd. I was looking for a place where we could cut a door in the trailer. A Thor door." He pointed to a place at the bottom of the wall. "That seems to be about the only place we could make it."

Thor came in about an hour later, and Todd finally got to bed.

A few days after they returned home, Dad carefully cut a small hole in the side of the trailer and hung a little swinging door in the space. Thor didn't wait for the next camping trip but immediately started going in and out as he chose.

A few nights later, Todd couldn't find Thor at bedtime.

"I know where he is," Molly yelled. "He's in the trailer waiting to go camping."

"I'll go check," Todd said, feeling certain Molly was right. But Thor wasn't in the trailer. Todd clomped back to the house feeling discouraged.

Molly had gone to bed. Mom and Dad had divided up the newspaper and quietly read in the living room. The house felt as silent as a church. Todd decided to get a drink of milk and then go on to bed. If Thor wanted to spend the night outdoors, who cared? The nights were warm now.

Todd took his milk to the breakfast bar and sipped it slowly. He had to smile as he thought about his pet. He knew the cat still considered him its mother. But sometimes it acted like a spoiled brat.

Slowly a tiny sound registered on Todd's brain. He could barely hear the fascinating sound, but he moved toward it, forgetting all about Thor. As he moved toward the end of the kitchen, the sound became ever so slightly louder. He stopped and listened again. It sounded like chewing and seemed to be coming from the cabinet over the stove. Todd noticed the cabinet door over the stove stood ajar. They had never had a mouse in the house, but the noise certainly sounded like chewing.

Todd wanted to open the cupboard, but somehow he felt afraid. What would he do if a mouse jumped out? He knew he couldn't hurt one of the little creatures, but would one hurt him?

Todd stood in the silent kitchen listening to the tiny chewing sounds. Something alive was definitely making those sounds. Maybe he should get Dad. No, he wasn't some kind of baby. He would just step over to that door and open it. If something wanted to escape, he would open the sliding glass door and let it outside.

With that decision made, he reached up to the cabinet door. But he didn't open it. He stepped back and listened to the chewing, which definitely came from inside that door. And in the quiet, it almost sounded crunchy.

Todd squared his shoulders and reached for the door. He would open it quickly before he had a chance to change his mind.

He touched the handle and gently pulled the door open. But he didn't find a little animal. A big animal sat in the cupboard with its black face in a cookie bag. The crunching suddenly sounded so loud in the silent room that Todd felt sure Mom and Dad would hear and come running.

"Thor!" Todd whispered. "What are you doing in those cookies?" The cat pulled his head from the bag, looked down at Todd, and said "Mew" as softly as a little kitten.

Todd laughed out loud. "I'm coming," it sounded like Thor had said. "Can't you just wait until I finish my bedtime snack?"

Todd snatched Thor from the cupboard, cookie bag and all, and set them outside on the patio. Then he washed his hands, ran some water into the sink, poured in a little dishwashing soap, and thoroughly washed the cabinet Thor had been in and the countertops below. He would have to watch that bad cat and keep him out of there. Dad wouldn't think it was all that much better to have cats in the cupboards than mice.

Thor plays a song on the piano.

# CHAPTER
# 9

# Run Over!

Todd didn't want Dad to know that Thor had been into the cupboards. When Thor finished eating, Todd threw the rest of the cookies into the garbage can. After checking to see that the kitchen looked all right, he scooped up the cat and hurried to bed.

With school out, Todd had been sleeping in a little each morning. The next morning after the cookie incident, as Todd dozed, trying to wake up, he heard Molly scream, "Mommy! Come quick. Come see what Thor's doing."

Instantly awake, Todd jumped into his clothes, expecting to find Thor in the cupboard again. He forgot that the cookies were already in Thor's tummy or the garbage can. Following Molly's excited voice, Todd found himself in the utility room bathroom. When he peeked through the open door, Thor ran between his feet toward the kitchen.

"You're too late!" Molly yelled. "I wanted you and Mommy to see what Thor did."

Mom arrived about that time. "OK, why don't you tell us what Thor did," she asked with a smile. "Was it good or bad?"

"It was good," Molly said. "He went potty in the toilet."

"Come on," Todd said. "He probably just walked across the seat."

"No, he didn't, Todd. I saw him."

Todd grinned. "Did he flush it?"

"All right," Mom said, "let's forget it and go eat."

After breakfast, Todd and Molly worked in the garden. While the kids pulled weeds from around the plants, Thor found the catnip poking through the ground. He rolled over and over in it. When he finished, the little catnip patch looked as though some monster had trampled it. Todd knew the plants would be all right in a few days. But he straightened them up the best he could anyway.

That evening Dad asked Todd to help him fertilize the garden. As they stepped into the garage, a tiny gray-brown mouse ran under the edge of the fertilizer bag.

"Let's try to herd it outside," Dad said. Todd stood a few feet from Dad and walked slowly toward the big open door. But the mouse didn't want to go outside. It ran between Todd's feet to the back of the garage and behind the freezer.

"I'm sorry, Todd," Dad said, "but we can't have a mouse in here. The next thing we know it will run into the house. Mice don't do any harm outside, but when they get inside they do a lot of damage as well as spread filth. Go get Thor."

Todd gulped then ran after Thor.

"Shove him behind the freezer," Dad said.

Todd did. Thor gladly started investigating. A moment later he jumped out with the mouse squeaking in his mouth. Todd's mouth went dry. He thought about how he would feel if he were in a big monster's mouth.

Thor brought the mouse away from the freezer, dropped it to the floor, and started chirping to it, exactly like a mother cat chirps to her kitten. Each time the mouse tried to run away, Thor chirped again and gently put it back.

A wide smile covered Dad's face. "Thor thinks the mouse is a kitten."

Todd felt the big lump in his throat growing smaller. "Do you think he'll hurt it?" he asked.

Dad shook his head. "When a cat makes that sound, you know he isn't going to hurt it. Come on, let's go feed the plants. I guarantee Thor and the mouse will be here when we finish."

Todd could hardly stand spreading the white stuff around the plants while he knew that poor little mouse was squeaking in terror.

When they finished the last row of beans, Todd took off running, leaving Dad to gather up the tools they had used. He stopped when he reached the garage. What if Thor had hurt the mouse? He swallowed and forced himself to go on into the garage. He looked around—but neither Thor nor the mouse was anywhere to be seen.

Dad rushed into the garage and dropped the big blue bucket onto the concrete floor. Then he met Todd's eyes and grinned. "Where are they?"

"I can't find them, Dad."

"Thor must have gotten bored and gone into the house. The mouse probably decided to take off." Dad thought a minute. "I hope Thor didn't take the mouse inside." He hurried into the house.

Todd decided to look outside, so he walked around, calling Thor's name. The sun had dropped behind the hills, and deep shadows filled the yard. Todd walked past a squatty bush, calling Thor's name. He heard something. But what was it? Then he heard a tiny sound in a shrub. Todd walked to the big bush, lifted its droopy branches, and looked under it. Thor lay there, curled up with the mouse tucked against his tummy. But when the cat looked up at Todd, the mouse jumped right over Thor's side and ran into the darkness.

"Good boy!" Todd said happily. "You didn't hurt it."

"I'm glad he got the mouse outside without hurting it," Dad said later. "It's a shame to hurt God's creatures."

Thor awakened Todd several times that night, chirping as though to a baby kitten.

Todd awakened one morning to find Thor gone. Jumping into his clothes, he hurried down the hall to the bathroom. He started to go in, when he noticed Thor on the toilet. A tiny sound like water dripping reached Todd's ears. A moment later Thor jumped off and ran down the hall.

"Mom! " Todd yelled. "Molly was right. Thor is using the toilet. I just saw him do it!" Molly shouted with glee. Now Todd believed her.

The annual church campout took place that weekend, and, of course, the Keane family would go. Mom and the kids packed the trailer before Dad got home from work.

"Everything's ready," Mom called. "Why don't you go out and hook up the trailer, Todd?"

Far too young to drive on the road, Todd loved to move the pickup around on their property. Mom didn't have to ask him twice.

He hopped into the big pickup, pushed the key into the ignition, and turned it. It felt so good to be driving. He turned and checked carefully behind the truck. Nothing there. Putting it into reverse, he eased slowly back toward the trailer.

"Stop!" Molly screamed. Todd jammed the brake pedal to the floor. "Todd, stop! You ran over Thor!" Todd jumped from the pickup to find his pet lying in front of the back wheel on the passenger side. The big cat looked dead. Suddenly the world looked blacker than Todd had ever seen it.

Is there any hope for poor Thor?

# CHAPTER

# *10*

## Thor Goes to the Hospital

As Todd knelt beside his beloved Thor, Mom came racing around the side of the house. "Molly said you ran over Thor," she puffed.

Todd felt too choked up to talk. He nodded, gazing at the still form. Suddenly he saw the little chest move up and down— ever so slightly. "He's breathing, Mom!"

"Get a cardboard box," she said softly.

Todd had the box almost before Mom finished asking for it. He peeled off his green knit shirt and spread it in the bottom while Molly watched helplessly. "There. Let's use all six of our hands to put him in.

We don't want to hurt him any more."

Mom, Todd, and Molly carefully slid their hands under the soft little body and ever so gently lifted him into the box.

As they approached the car, Todd spoke through clenched teeth. "I'm never going to drive again." He climbed in the front seat beside Mom with the precious box cradled on his lap. Molly jumped into the back.

No one spoke for a while. Molly wiped her eyes and nose on her sleeve. She leaned forward. "Mommy," she whimpered, "it wasn't Todd's fault. He backed really slow, but Thor was lying right behind the wheel. Todd couldn't see him, Mommy." She started sniffing again as she thought about it.

Mom reached her hand back and patted Molly. "I know, sweetie. It's just one of those things."

Todd didn't take his eyes off his pet. "Hey," he suddenly shouted, "he opened his eyes." But before Todd finished reporting it, the cat's eyes closed again as if he'd sunk peacefully into a deep sleep.

The twelve miles to the vet seemed to go on forever, but they finally got there. The receptionist took them right into the examining room, and the doctor came in immediately. He examined Thor and took several X-rays before he turned to the anxious family. "Your cat is pretty thoroughly crushed," he said. "He has internal injuries and many broken bones. His chances are minimal, but if you want me to try, I'll do what I can. Right now, I can only treat him for shock."

"Do what you can, Doctor," Mom said. "He's a beloved member of our family." Then she put her arms around Todd and Molly and steered them through the glass doors.

As they drove back home, no one said a word. When they unlocked the front door, they filed silently into the living room. Still no one spoke.

In a few minutes Dad's car tires crunched over the gravel driveway. Then they heard Dad's jolly voice. "Hello! Are we all ready to go? Hello? Hey, is anyone home?"

"We're in here, Daddy," Molly called.

As Dad walked into the living room, Molly threw herself into his arms and cried. "Daddy, Thor's hurt really, really bad. He's at the vet's, and he may die!" She buried her face in his shoulder and wept bitterly.

Dad hugged her tightly and looked at Mom with a big question in his eyes. She told him the details. "Should we go ahead with the campout?" she asked. "It would keep the kids' minds busy over the weekend."

"No!" Todd said. "No, we can't go anywhere. We have to stay right here where we can know how Thor is." Molly agreed through her sobs and tears.

Dad gave a small sigh. "OK, we'll stay home. We wouldn't enjoy the trip anyway."

The whole family pitched in and made potato soup for supper, but no one could eat.

"It's nearly sundown," Dad called soon after the dishes were finished. "Let's go ahead and have worship."

As the family collected their Bibles and settled down, Molly scooted over to Mom. "Mommy," she said so softly she almost whispered, "can we pray for Thor? Don't you think Jesus loves little cats?"

Mom looked at Dad, and Dad looked at Mom. Because they knew Thor lay near death, they felt afraid to pray. They didn't want Todd and Molly to be disappointed if Jesus answered No to their prayers.

"I'll tell you what," Dad answered after some time. "Let's go ahead with our regular worship. Then we'll see if we can find anything in the Bible to help us decide if we can pray for our kitty."

They read their usual two chapters in the Bible, but Todd and Molly asked to skip the songs and Bible game. They also asked to have prayer later. With Dad leading, they all sat around the table, searching the Bible, with the help of the concordance.

After a while, they sat back in their chairs as Dad told what they had found. "We haven't found a text that says 'Pray for your pets.' But we found one that says He sees a sparrow fall and several that say if we pray with faith, He'll give us what we ask. And some that say He likes to give us good gifts."

Both kids jumped to their feet. "Let's

pray for Thor," Todd said.

Everyone knelt, and God never heard more sincere, heartfelt prayers. And they were all for one little cat.

After praying, Dad suggested that they read a book together to help the time go faster. "It's going to be a long, long weekend," he added.

The kids went upstairs to the library and returned with a book called *Detective Zack and the Secret of Noah's Flood*. They started taking turns reading a page at a time.

After an hour, Molly finished her page and closed the book. "I want to pray for Thor again," she said. "May we?"

They all prayed again. Then Dad yawned. "We may as well go to bed now. We won't hear anything more tonight."

Todd thought he wouldn't sleep a wink, but he finally did.

Mom and Dad had breakfast ready the next morning when he staggered to the kitchen. After they ate, Mom suggested they skip Sabbath School but go to church.

Stony silence met her suggestion. After

a long pause, Todd picked up the telephone and handed it to Mom. "Call the vet," he pleaded. "He may know something by now."

Mom called and murmured a few words. "I see. Yes, I know. I'm sure you are." Finally she thanked the doctor and hung up. Tears glistened in her eyes as she faced her family. "Thor's really bad," she whispered. "The doctor told me to prepare you for—" she sniffed as if she couldn't finish— "to prepare you for the worst," she finally sobbed.

"But he doesn't know we're praying," Molly said.

"Is the vet trying to help Thor?" Dad asked.

Mom shook her head. "He's giving him only intravenous feeding and painkillers. He said that's all he can do right now." She broke down and sobbed for a moment then raised her face. "He says Thor has so many broken bones he doesn't know how he would ever put him back together."

Thor, the miracle cat.

# CHAPTER
# *11*

# Thor's Special Miracle

"We'd better pray," Dad said softly when Mom said that the vet had no hope for Thor.

Another prayer session left everyone reaching for tissues. Then they read some more about Zack, the boy who found clues that Noah's flood really happened. The book got so interesting that they read for two hours. Then they went for a walk in the woods. Finding a shady spot under a tree, they prayed again.

They all helped fix lunch. Then they prayed again. They read awhile then prayed yet again.

After sundown, Todd begged Mom to call the doctor. When she hung up, she looked awful. "He's not even a little better." She sobbed.

Todd slid to his knees. "The Bible tells us if we ask, believing, God will answer our prayers. It also says He wants to give us good gifts, and He made the animals for us. Well, I believe, so come on."

No one mentioned TV that Saturday evening. The family continued reading and praying until bedtime.

The next morning, Mom called the vet again—with the same response. "He's barely alive. Probably the food and liquid going into his veins by IV are all that's keeping him going at all."

Molly told them it was time for them to pray—and to believe God would make their pet well. She and Todd dropped to their knees. Mom and Dad looked into each other's tortured eyes, shrugged, and kneeled too.

After prayer, Dad asked Todd to vacuum the floors and Molly to do the dishes. Then the family walked in the woods, prayed, and read.

They finished the book at two-thirty. Todd took it back to the library. "The Bible says we have to have faith," he said when he returned. "I'm worried about our faith. Let's pray one more time. Let's pray again, believing Thor will be healed." Dad opened his mouth to say something and then stopped. They all prayed together.

A few minutes before three, the phone rang. Mom answered as the rest listened. "Hello," she said in a quivery voice. Suddenly she was crying so hard she could barely speak. "Oh, Dr. Grimes," she finally managed to say, "you didn't make a mistake. Believe me, you didn't. We'll tell you when we come."

When she hung up, she looked up through heavy tears and grabbed both children to her. "He's OK! He's all right! He got better really fast about an hour ago, so Dr. Grimes decided to try to set some of his broken bones. He took more X-rays, and Thor doesn't have one broken bone." She sobbed again.

"Well, honey," Dad said, rubbing her

shoulders, "the kids sure taught us something about faith this weekend."

A moment later, they all fell to their knees again. Laughing and crying together, they thanked their heavenly Father for healing their precious little pet.

Then they all climbed into the car to go after Thor.

Todd and Molly talked at the same time as they told Dr. Grimes about their weekend of prayer. The man smiled gently then reached for a tissue. He wiped his eyes then blew his nose. "I knew you folks loved that cat a lot," he said. "It really hurt me when I couldn't help him. But I want you to know that you've made a believer out of me. God healed him, and that's a fact. There's no other way your cat could have lived."

"We know God healed him too," Molly said. "We prayed all the time."

The doctor nodded. "I hope you'll handle Thor very gently for a few days." He passed his hand over his chin and grinned. "I know he's healed. I saw both sets of X-rays. But surely the cat has to be sore. Just be careful with him."

Dad reached for Dr. Grimes's hand. "We'll treat him like a king," he said. "Thanks, Doctor."

Todd felt higher than a cloud as Dad drove home. He held Thor on his lap, the big brown cat purring and pumping his feet against Todd's legs.

"Do you think Thor's still sore?" Molly asked. She leaned over the front seat to talk to her parents.

Mom looked back and patted Molly's hand. "He may be, Molly. We'll baby him up a lot—just in case. OK?"

Molly sighed. "OK. But Jesus healed him, didn't He?" She sighed again. "Do you think Jesus would heal him and leave him sore?"

"Thor's going to live," Todd muttered, petting the cat's nose with his finger. "We'll just act as if he's sore. Then we won't hurt him."

Molly leaned back, thinking.

When they got home, Todd carried the cat in and laid him on the couch. "Let's thank Jesus again for making Thor well," he said. Everyone gladly got to their knees and held hands. Then each one thanked God and told Him how much they loved Him.

"Let's talk a little about how God heals," Dad said when they'd settled back on the couch and chairs.

"I know how He does it," Molly chirped. "He just says it, and the healing happens."

Dad smiled. "He certainly can. But did you know that God heals you every time you skin your knee?" He nodded. "If He didn't, your knee would never heal. You'd just get more sores and scrapes until they covered your whole body. Sometimes He heals slowly. You get better each day. But that's still God healing you."

"I never thought of that," Todd said.

Dad nodded again. "I know. We don't appreciate His healing until He does something big. But sometimes, even when He heals someone who's seriously ill, He does it gradually. The person just starts to get better until he's well." He looked at each one of his family. "That's a miracle too. As much as the one we've just seen." He stretched and got up. "I'm hungry. Who's ready to help me make supper?"

All three jumped to their feet. Everyone felt starved. After all, they had barely eaten for two days.

Everyone treated Thor as if he were sore, but he didn't know it. He ran and played as usual.

"We don't have to treat Thor special anymore," Molly said the next evening at the supper table. "He's just as well as I am."

Todd grinned. "Wrong, Molly. We have to treat him special forever. If God thought he was worth healing, then he must be a special cat."

Everyone laughed. Then Dad sobered up. "I think you might be a little wrong, too, Todd. I know God made and loves Thor, but I wonder if He could have healed Thor because He loves you two so awfully much. After all, He died for you. And you're going to live forever—with Him."

Everyone agreed. "That's right," Mom said. "Even so, Thor will always be special to us. When we look at him, we'll remember how much God cares about every little thing."

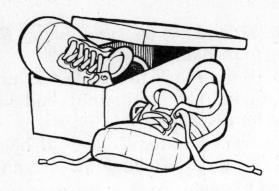

## Whoever said the Bible was boring didn't know about The Shoebox Kids

Inspired by the series of stories in Primary Treasure by Jerry D. Thomas, The Shoebox Kids book series has been helping children like yours understand the lessons of the Bible for years.

Following the adventures of Chris, Maria, DeeDee, Willie, Jenny, and Sammy in these books is more than just fun—it leads to new discoveries about what the Bible really means at home, at school, or on the playground.

If your child wants to be a friend of Jesus, The Shoebox Kids books are just for you.

**Get each one.**
Paperback. US$6.99, Can$9.99 each.
Available at your local ABC. Call 1-800-765-6955 to order.

Book 1 - *The Case of the Secret Code*
    Topic: Prayer. 0-8163-1249-4
Book 2 - *The Mysterious Treasure Map*
    Topic: Baptism. 0-8163-1256-7
Book 3 - *Jenny's Cat-napped Cat*
    Topic: Forgiveness. 0-8163-1277-X
Book 4 - *The Missing Combination Mystery*
    Topic: Jealousy. 0-8163-1276-1
Book 5 - *The Broken Dozen Mystery*
    Topic: Helping others. 0-8163-1332-6
Book 6 - *The Wedding Dress Disaster*
    Topic: Commitment. 0-8163-1355-5
Book 7 - *The Clue in the Secret Passage*
    Topic: Bible. 0-8163-1386-5
Book 8 - *The Rockslide Rescue*
    Topic: Trust in God. 0-8163-1387-3
Book 9 - *The Secret of the Hidden Room*
    Topic: Prejudice. 0-8163-1682-1
Book 10 - *Adventure on Wild Horse Mountain*
    Topic: Judging Others. 0-8163-1683-X

# Animal Stories
# the Whole Family Can Enjoy!

It all started with a perfectly pesky pet parrot named Julius and his pal Mitch. Then came a rascally red fox, a wildly wacky raccoon, a curiously comical cow, and a thunder cat by the name of Thor! But all of them help kids celebrate God's creation with laughter and wonder. Collect the entire "herd' and get a belly laugh or two yourself from the **Julius & Friends** series.

Paperback. US$6.99, Can$9.99 each.

Book 1 - *Julius, the Perfectly Pesky Pet Parrot*. 0-8163-1173-0
Book 2 - *Julius Again!* 0-8163-1239-7
Book 3 - *Tina, the Really Rascally Red Fox*. 0-8163-1321-0
Book 4 - *Skeeter, the Wildly Wacky Raccoon*. 0-8163-1388-1
Book 5 - *Lucy, the Curiously Comical Cow*. 0-8163-1582-5
Book 6 - *Thor, the Thunder Cat*. 0-8163-1703-8

**Available at your local ABC. Call 1-800-765-6955 to order.**